some people throw birdseed

Thanks to all the beautiful brides,
because they make us dream.
Thanks to all the funny brides,
because they make us smile.
— B. M.

To all the little girls who dream
of a fairy-tale wedding dress.
— A. L. C.

First published in the United States in 2003
by Watson-Guptill Publications,
a division of VNU Business Media, Inc.
770 Broadway, New York, NY 10003
www.watsonguptill.com

Library of Congress Control Number: 2002010578
ISBN: 0-8230-1738-9

First published in Italy in 2002
by Edizioni Arka, Milan

1 2 3 4 5 6 7 8 / 10 09 08 07 06 05 04 03

US: Machine wash, cold, delicate cycle. **No bleach.**
Warm iron. No dryclean. No tumble dry.

© Edizioni Arka, 2002
Printed in Italy
First printing, 2002

The Wedding Dress Mess

A story by Beatrice Masini
Illustrations by Anna Laura Cantone
Text adaptation by Lenny Hort

marie
CATALOGUE
IDEAS
MODA

Wedding

Watson-Guptill Publications
New York

Filomena was the finest seamstress in Italy. She made the snazziest skirts, the sassiest sportswear, the splashiest swimsuits. But her wedding dresses were the icing on the cake.

All the brides for miles around said, "Filomena, I want to be the most beautiful bride!"

And Filomena never let them down.

SWIMSUIT

WEDDING

DRESS

ACKE T

T-SHIRT

FASHION
DESIGNER

CLOTHING

WEDDING
abito   da   sposa
DRESS

total-look

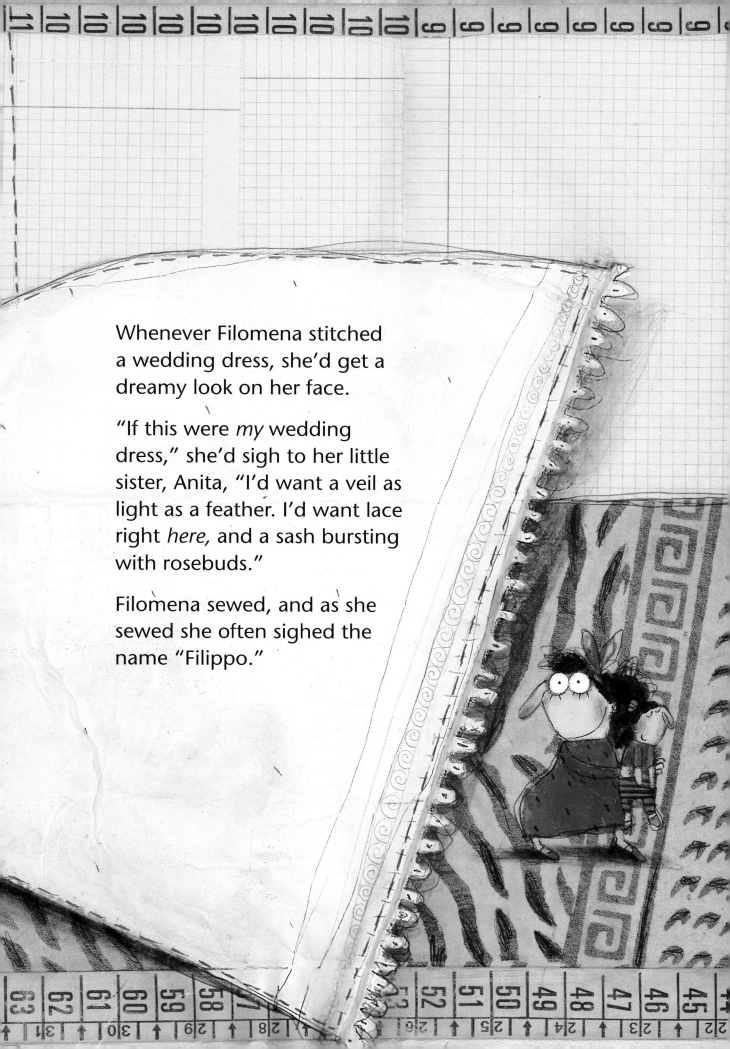

Whenever Filomena stitched a wedding dress, she'd get a dreamy look on her face.

"If this were *my* wedding dress," she'd sigh to her little sister, Anita, "I'd want a veil as light as a feather. I'd want lace right *here,* and a sash bursting with rosebuds."

Filomena sewed, and as she sewed she often sighed the name "Filippo."

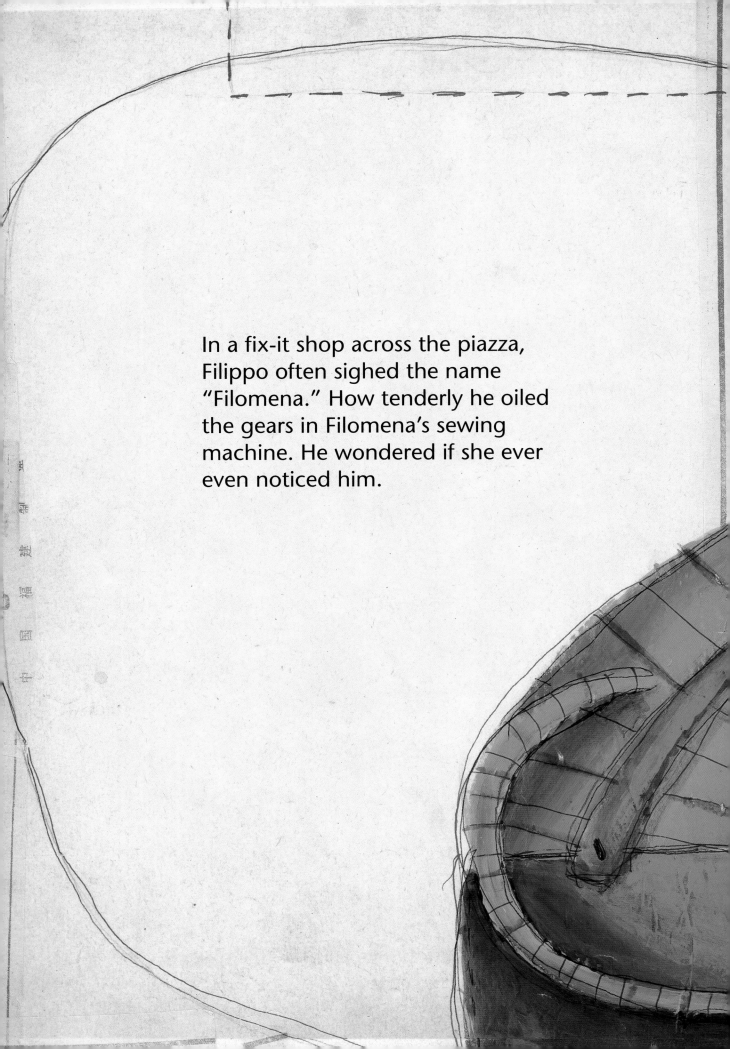

In a fix-it shop across the piazza, Filippo often sighed the name "Filomena." How tenderly he oiled the gears in Filomena's sewing machine. He wondered if she ever even noticed him.

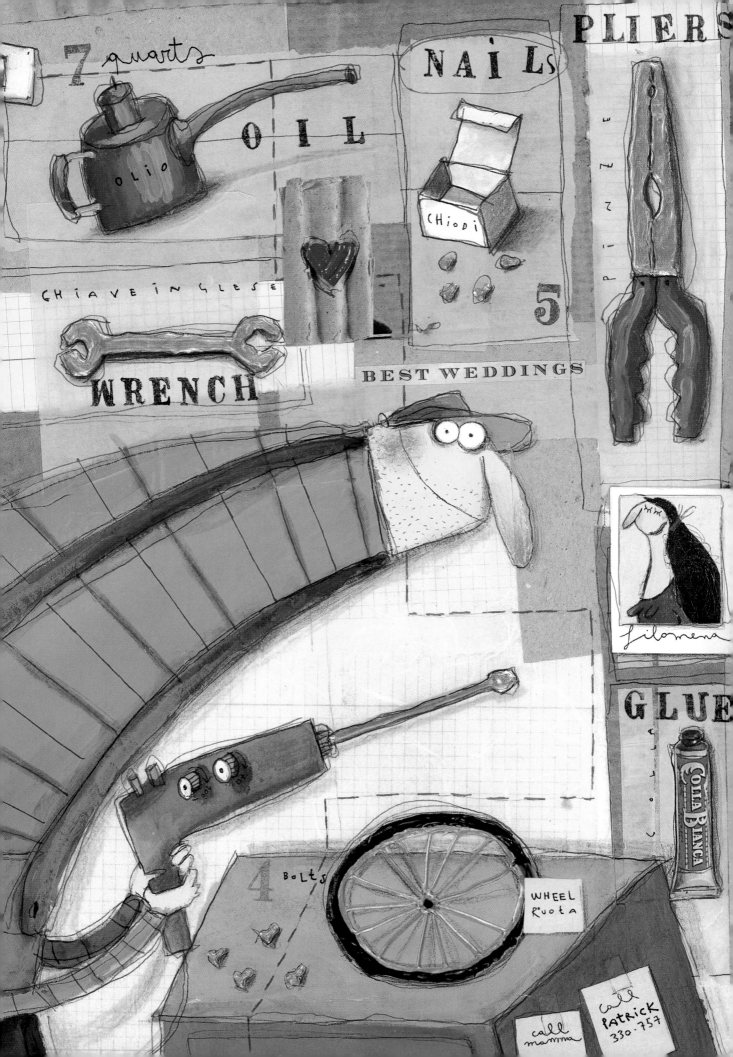

UN GIORNO SPECIALE

One day, after many dreams and many sighs, Filippo gathered up his courage and stood before Filomena's balcony.

"Filomena, I...I...I love you," he shyly sputtered. "Will you, will you...?"

Filomena gazed deeply into his eyes and said, "I'll start on my wedding dress right away."

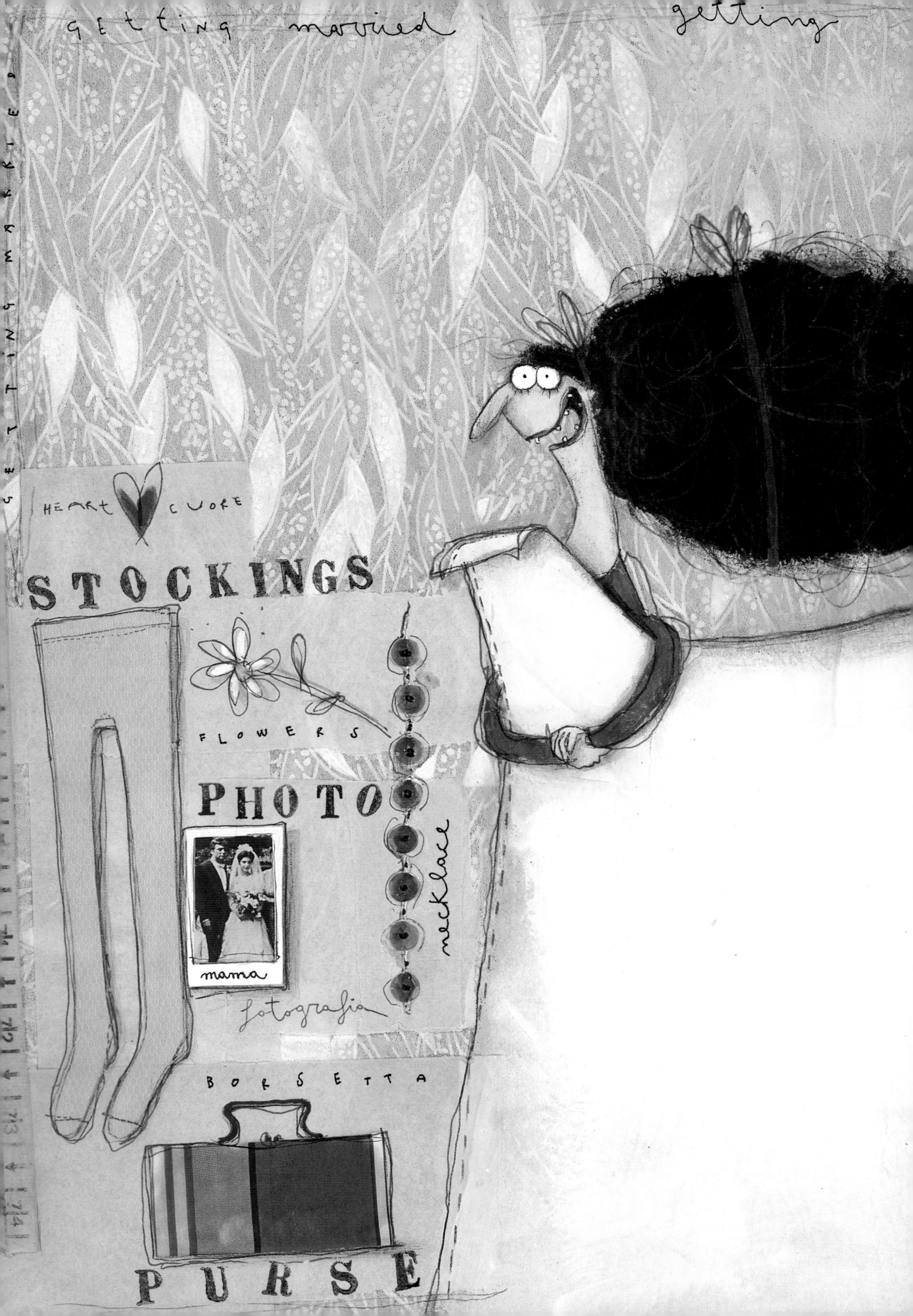

getting married
getting
HEART CUORE
STOCKINGS
FLOWERS
PHOTO
mama
fotografia
necklace
BORSETTA
PURSE

Filomena had been imagining
her dress for a long time. She had
enough ideas to fill the Colosseum.

SEAMSTRESS

cucitrice

Every Sunday Filippo would drop by with his-and-her crash helmets and invite his beloved for a romantic ride in the country.

"I'd love to," she'd say, "but you go without me. I have to work on my wedding dress."

So poor Filippo would ride that romantic countryside all by himself. He couldn't wait until the two of them were married and the dress was finally done with.

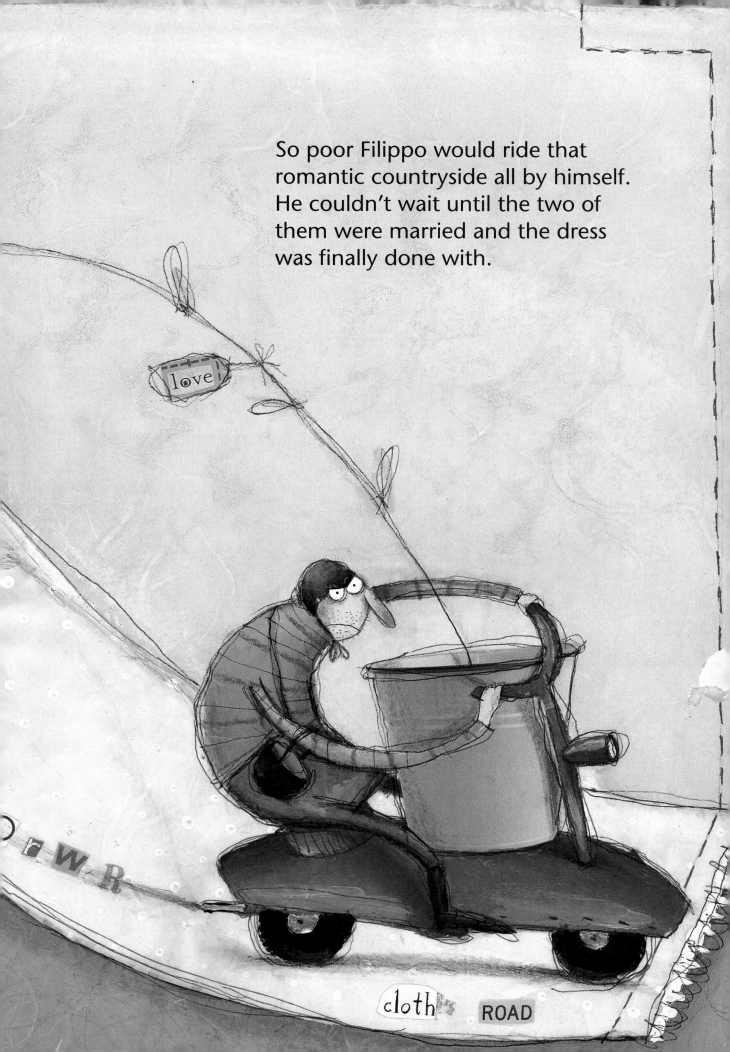

The happy day arrived at last. The village church was packed with excited people, all waiting for a glimpse of Filomena's masterpiece.

Filippo waited blissfully on the church steps in his stylish green suit.

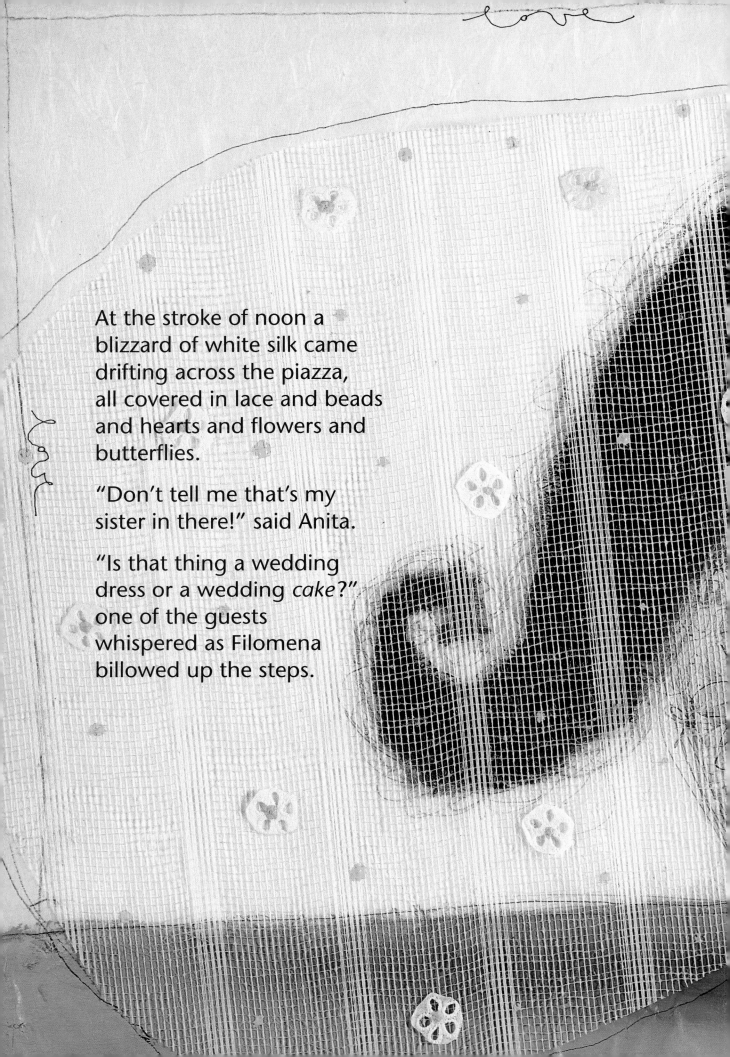

At the stroke of noon a
blizzard of white silk came
drifting across the piazza,
all covered in lace and beads
and hearts and flowers and
butterflies.

"Don't tell me that's my
sister in there!" said Anita.

"Is that thing a wedding
dress or a wedding *cake*?"
one of the guests
whispered as Filomena
billowed up the steps.

I am a Princess

LOVE

almost married

Somebody snorted, somebody giggled, somebody chuckled, and soon the whole church was ringing with laughter.

Filippo panicked and bolted out the side door.

Suddenly everything was quiet except
for the *putt-putt* of Filippo's scooter.

"Angel!" cried Filomena. She threw back
her veil and scooted right after him.

She hustled out of her bustle. She kicked off her high-heeled shoes and yanked off her fluttering veil. Lace and beads and feathers and flowers scattered helter-skelter through the streets as Filomena sprinted after the runaway groom.

CHURCH

START 1

TEA PARTY 2

A WEDDING GIFT

advance 3 spaces

3

Lose your

shoes.....

DICE

CHICKEN crossing 5

4

lose a turn

flowers

6

With a glorious burst of speed, she caught up to him near the edge of town.

"I'm sorry I let a silly dress come between us," she said.

"I'm sorry I ran away," he said.

"I'm ready for that romantic ride in the country," she said.

"Maybe we should go back to the church first," he said.

So they were married after all, Filippo in his stylish green suit…

And Filomena in
her simple white dress.

Everyone agreed she was the
most beautiful bride they had ever seen.